My 100 Hands

To: Mavis

by Lauryn Marie Burks

Lauryn ♡ A!!

Illustrations by Alexandra Hananel

www.My100Hands.com

My 100 Hands
by Lauryn Marie Burks
Illustrations by Alexandra Hananel
www.My100Hands.com

Published by Munchkin Power, LLC
6801 Oak Hall Ln
Suite 761
Columbia, MD 21045
www.munchkinpowerllc.com

ISBN: 978-0-9883252-0-3

Printed in the United States of America

I wish I had 100 hands to do whatever I want them to.

Oh my goodness! It is my 100 hands!

2

"I am Helpful Hand, Lauryn.
My job is to teach good manners
to you and all of your friends."

"Hello! My name is Happy Hand.
I am going to make sure that everyone
has a positive attitude and lots of fun!"

"Hi, darling! I am Pretty Hand. My job is to remind boys and girls that they are special!"

"Now, Lauryn, what may we do for you?"

I could get dressed for school easier if I had 100 hands. They could help me put lotion on my back where I cannot reach.

My 100 hands could help snap my dresses when Mommy and Daddy are busy.

When I clean up my room, my 100 hands could put away things that go really high up.

My 100 hands could help me paint my room and put up curtains too!

My 100 hands could help fix
my breakfast before school. If I spill
my milk, the hands will help me clean up. 11

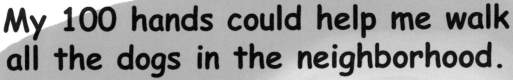

My 100 hands could help me walk
all the dogs in the neighborhood.

13

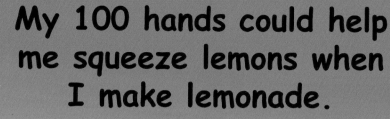

My 100 hands could help me squeeze lemons when I make lemonade.

My 100 hands could help me count to one million!

My 100 hands could fly too!

My 100 hands could fly
all the way up to
heaven.

I wish I had 100 hands! I am going to ask my daddy to buy them for me.

The End

Create-A-Hand

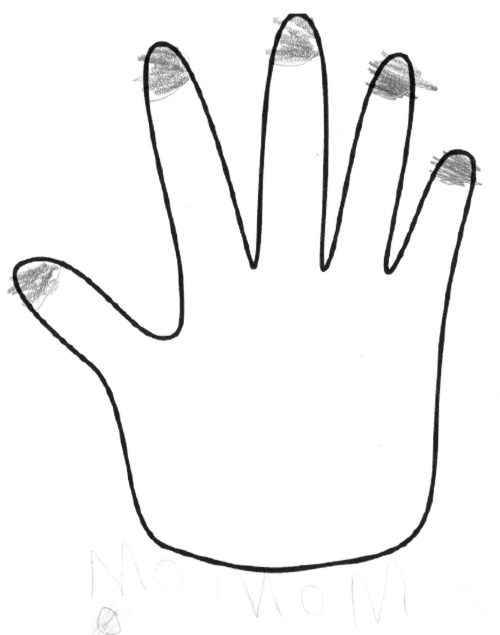

Use this space to create a new hand

Create-A-Hand

MAVIS'S HAND

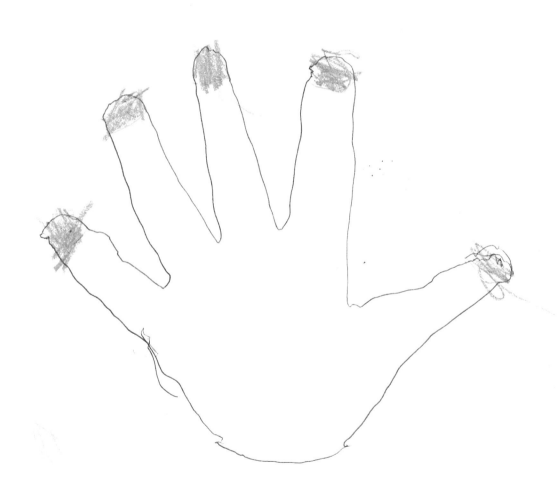

Use this space to create a new hand

About the Author

Lauryn Marie Burks

Lauryn Marie Burks is a bright, articulate, imaginative child. She loves participating in Children's Church, reading books, singing songs, dancing and watching her favorite movies. An aspiring actress, she is not shy about making new experiences, and she is warm and friendly to everyone she meets.

This story, *My 100 Hands*, was created by Lauryn, when she was just just 5 years old. While faced with the constant challenge of staying on task and dealing with hurried parents, Lauryn day-dreamed about having 100 friendly little hands that would help her perform various tasks and chores. As the word spreads, Lauryn is being called upon to do group readings with her peers, and teachers are requesting copies of books to share with students. People are amazed that a child so young is the author of a children's book. They will be more amazed when they learn that she has already started her second book of the series, called *My 100 Hands Go To School*.

**Harness the creative energy
and ideas of your kid! Visit our
website and share your kid's
amazing accomplishments.**

www.munchkinpowerllc.com

CPSIA information can be obtained at www.ICGtesting.com
Printed in the USA
BVIW12n2234080716
454867BV00001B/2